# Scrapbooks of America™

**Published by Tradition Books® and distributed to the school and library market by The Child's World®**
P.O. Box 326, Chanhassen, MN 55317-0326 — **800/599-READ** — *http://www.childsworld.com*

**Photo Credits:** Cover: Bettmann/Corbis; Buffalo Bill Historical Center/McCracken Research Library: 18, 24, 25, 28, 39; Ansel Adams Publishing Rights Trust/Corbis: 30; James L. Amos/Corbis: 40; Bettmann/Corbis: 6, 12, 17, 34; Corbis: 15, 32, 35, 38; Denver Public Library/Colorado Historical Society and Denver Museum: 7; Stock Montage: 9, 10, 11, 13, 16, 22, 23

**An Editorial Directions book**
Editorial Directions, Inc.: E. Russell Primm, Editorial Director; Lucia Raatma, Line Editor, Photo Selector, and Additional Writing; Katie Marsico, Assistant Editor; Olivia Nellums, Editorial Assistant; Susan Hindman, Copy Editor; Susan Ashley, Proofreader; Alice Flanagan, Photo Researcher and Additional Writer

Design: The Design Lab

**Library of Congress Cataloging-in-Publication Data**
Cataloging-in-Publication data for this title has been applied for and is available from the United States Library of Congress.

*Scrapbooks of America*™

# TAG-ALONG TAY

## A Story about Annie Oakley and Buffalo Bill's Wild West Show

by Pamela Dell

TRADITION BOOKS®

*A New Tradition in Children's Publishing*™

MAPLE PLAIN, MINNESOTA

t a b l e   o f   c o n t e n t s

"Come on, come on, come on! Move it, Tay. Let's go!" My brother, Jeremiah, hollered at me over his shoulder from up ahead. Jem, as I called him, was impatient. But the crowd was **suffocating** me as it pushed forward, squashing me from all sides. I was lost in a boiling mass of bodies pressing in toward the entrance gate in the early July heat, and I was doing poorly at keeping up.

"Jem, wait!" I called to him, hoping not to sound too frantic.

He stopped then, hands on hips, and the crowd flowed around him like a river flows around a big rock. He was nineteen-years-old big—and sturdy enough not to get knocked around at all. At twelve, I was

Posters like these got many of us excited about seeing Buffalo Bill and his show.

Aspen was a quiet place compared to the big city of Chicago.

big for my age, too. But not big enough to keep a human **herd** of buffalo from pushing me all over the place. They weren't paying any attention to me at all. That was because every one of them was bent on getting into that **arena** and grabbing the best possible seat at the show. Especially Jem.

Coming from the little town of Aspen, Colorado, neither Jem nor I had ever spent much time in crowds. So it troubled me badly to be in the middle of such a herd. But a pushy pack of people didn't give Jem a moment's worry. He was pushy, too. He went his own way always and never minded how many folks he had to shove through to get there.

At the moment, there was a look of real **annoyance** on his face. What he didn't like was having to stop and wait for me. I could see it plain as a thunder cloud as I caught up. Same as I'd seen it all the way from Aspen to Chicago.

"I guess you're planning to be Miss Tag-Along all the rest of your life, huh, Tay-girl?" Jem said, putting his hand around the back of my head and guiding me forward toward the entrance gate. I knew it was supposed to be playful big-brother teasing, but I didn't say a word in reply. I'd heard those words too many times already. If I said what I felt about it, we'd be arguing in no time flat, and my whole afternoon would be ruined.

In 1882, Buffalo Bill put on his first show. It was called the Old Glory Blowout and helped celebrate the Fourth of July in North Platte, Nebraska, where he was living at the time. His Wild West Show began the next year.

It wasn't so many months since we'd gone through Aspen's long, fearful winter with all its terrible happenings, and we'd come out the other side a family with nothing left but each other. If anything could take my mind off that fact, it was Colonel Buffalo Bill Cody's Wild West Show. I wasn't about to let anything spoil my experience of that, not even Jem's making fun.

Buffalo Bill's show was famous even as far away as Europe, and I'd waited a long time to get a chance to see it for myself. Plus, just a stone's toss away from the show arena was what Jem called the biggest event of the century: the Chicago World's Fair. Or, as

The Great Chicago Fire of 1871 destroyed much of the city. Hosting the Columbian Exposition in 1893 was one way for Chicago to show how well it had recovered.

The Columbian Exposition took up blocks and blocks, and its buildings had some amazing exhibits.

it was officially called, the Columbian Exposition, marking the 400-year anniversary of when Columbus first planted his boots in the New World.

I hadn't seen much of the fair yet, except its blocks of white marble buildings sparkling in the sunlight. But anyone could see it was a grand event. Those buildings housed **exhibits** from all over the world and every kind of new invention imaginable. But it was the Wild West Show that had my attention for the time being. It was the same for Jem. So I couldn't blame him for being impatient to get inside.

A day off was rare for him, and even more so for me. We had to work to pay for our rooms at the **boardinghouse** where we

There was a big crowd on opening day in 1893.

The Silver Queen was a silver statue of a beautiful girl. The people of Aspen sent the statue to the Columbian Exposition to generate support for silver currency.

A ticket to the Columbian Exposition

stayed. Jem of course had the finer job. I did laundry and mending, trying to fit my schooling in wherever I could. But he watched over the awesome Silver Queen in the Mines and Mining Building, right on the fairgrounds. I couldn't often tag along there, which no doubt suited him just fine.

"Pass through, pass through," the man at the gate said when he saw my ticket. I turned and looked up at Jem, excited. He winked and threw me a boastful smile.

"You see, Tay-girl?" he said. "Didn't I tell you these cards would get us free seats at the finest entertainment this side of China?"

They had, too. Two shot-up playing cards, one for each of us, had got us in free of charge. Mine was a five of hearts, and each of those hearts was pierced by a small bullet hole. The best part was that the card was autographed by the person who had shot those holes there: Annie Oakley.

She was called a "champion **marks-woman**" on all the show posters I'd seen. Anyone who managed to get such a card always got in free to the Wild West Show. And Jem, just like always, had somehow managed it. Managed two, in fact. His was a black ace of spades, shot twice in the middle. Jem always had something working, always going after one thing or another.

I'd heard the arena could hold nearly

We couldn't wait to see Annie Oakley.

Buffalo Bill was not just a famous showman. During his lifetime, he was also a New York stage actor and served in the Nebraska legislature.

Buffalo Bill had such a presence! He was handsome as well as a fine horseman.

20,000 people, a number I couldn't imagine. But once we were inside, I knew I'd never been in a place so huge or with so many people all at once. Jem hustled us to seats in the middle and as far front as we could get. Once we were settled, I relaxed a bit and began to study the program.

It was billed as "Buffalo Bill's Wild West & **Congress** of Rough Riders of the World," with eighteen different events listed. Everything from bareback races to a buffalo hunt to a capture of the Deadwood Mail Coach, and more. I felt my heart pounding faster as the opening Grand Review began. Accompanied by a fine musical **hurrah,** a massive parade of horseback riders began to stream in from the end of the arena. I sucked in my breath as I caught sight of Buffalo Bill leading the way. Seeing him, the crowd came up on its feet like one big beast. Their cheers rose into the air, a long trumpet call of approval.

"Yee-haw!" Jem hooted and nudged me with his elbow. "He is something, isn't he? My future is right there, Tay!"

"Uh-huh." I nodded but didn't look at my brother. Buffalo Bill truly was something, with his beaded **buckskin** clothes and his long, flowing hair. He looked as wild and important and as brave as everybody said he was. Just like the hero he was in all those books about him. It wasn't any wonder the whole world went nuts scrambling to catch him in action.

Buffalo Bill's Wild West Show never portrayed Native Americans as savages, as some people thought of them. Instead, they were shown as talented riders.

The music lifted dramatically as the riders, many carrying flags, swarmed before our eyes. There were men of every skin color and wearing every type of costume a body could imagine. Indians, cowboys, and Mexican **vaqueros**—like nothing I'd ever seen in my life before. Jem whistled wildly as a band of Russian soldiers, called Cossacks, sped by waving **sabers.** So much action, my eyes could barely take it all in.

Buffalo Bill's spirited white horse rose up on its hind legs and whinnied. Bill raised his revolver in the air and shot twice,

The Wild West Show featured American Indians and people from all kinds of backgrounds.

straight up. Signaling the second act, I thought—the one I most wanted to see.

Jem turned to me again. "He likes to get the shooting going early," he pronounced, "so the ladies get accustomed to it. That's why Annie's coming up next."

I nodded, saying nothing. Sometimes Jem could be downright annoying. Especially when he acted like he knew every dang thing there ever was to know. But that was nothing compared to how I felt when he called me a tag-along. That I hated more than all the rest of his bad points put together.

I tried again to stop that train of dark thoughts from where it was heading though. Those winter thoughts, thoughts that were always trying to haunt me still, even months later.

Aspen had been hard hit. Raging snowstorms all season. **Avalanches** rumbling and roaring down the mountains like the fury of **archangels.** One avalanche worse than all the rest. That was the one that took our ma and pa when they were trying to make it back home to us one snow-covered late afternoon.

In the spring, the silver-mining company Jem worked for offered him a special job. He was asked to be part of the crew accompanying their Silver Queen to the World's Fair, where she'd be on display throughout July. With her silver body and golden crown, her hair of white glass and a scarf of pale blue crystals, she was the centerpiece of an awesome sculpture. She was meant to convince America to keep with

The Silver Queen was 18 feet (5.5 meters) tall and valued at about $20,000. What became of it after the fair remains an unsolved mystery.

The Silver Queen was a beautiful statue, and many people got to see it on display.

Annie Oakley sure knew how to put on a show.

the silver standard for money instead of changing to all gold. That mattered to folks in Aspen because silver mining was the one thing that kept our town alive.

Boy, if being chosen for that job didn't make Jem's chest puff all up. He was more than ready to get out of Aspen by then, too. His only problem was that he couldn't exactly leave me behind, orphaned and alone. He had no choice but for me to tag along, as he put it. Didn't take me any time at all to see that I was nothing but a stone around his neck, dragging him down.

All my unhappy memories flew like shadows before light the minute Annie Oakley was announced. I swooped to my feet with the rest of the crowd as she came fairly skipping into the arena, bowing and waving gracefully. Under her western-style hat, her dark hair hung loose at her shoulders instead of pinned up. I knew some people considered this highly improper for a lady. But if anyone in that crowd seemed to mind, it was impossible to tell for all the wild cheering they were doing. Jem stood, too. But although he clapped, he was above cheering for any girl.

I sat spellbound throughout Annie's whole performance, sure there were few women of her accomplishments. She was nearly as famous as Buffalo Bill himself, and some said she was a better shot, too. Watching her, I couldn't help but wonder

We weren't the only people who thought the Wild West Show was great.

what it would be like to be a famous performer facing a crowd this size.

I stole a glance at Jem. His profile was strong and still, and I felt he was sizing up the situation for himself as well. If he had half a chance, I knew he'd instantly trade in his Silver Queen job, glorious as it was, for a part in the Wild West Show. He no doubt meant to make that trade, no matter what would become of me. I turned back to watch Annie.

The first couple of times she fired, showing her skills with a rifle and a pistol, a few women in the audience screamed in fright. But as she went on with her exhibition, the wonder of it silenced everyone. It was clear why she was called Little Sure Shot, for the feats she performed were barely believable.

In less than half a minute, she'd blown more than a dozen glass balls to bits, after tossing each one into the air herself. And each trick after that was a new wonder. By the last of it, I felt I might burst just from seeing a person perform with such skill and grace. But even more because it was a fine lady doing the job, and not a man, the way things usually were.

Jem broke into my thoughts just as Annie's part of the show ended.

"Not too bad for a girl, huh, Tay?" he said as a storm of horseback riders and covered wagons streamed into the arena.

"You *wish* you could shoot so good, Jem," I replied.

"Well," he **drawled,** "if I rode along everywhere with Bill Cody, now I'm sure I'd pick up a few tricks, too."

"She didn't learn from him!" I blasted back. I knew all about Annie Oakley, as I'd read plenty. "She learned all on her own—when she was only eight years old! Why, by the time she was my age, she was even supporting her own poor family by hunting game and selling it to restaurants and such!"

George Custer's widow gave Buffalo Bill Cody permission to reenact her husband's defeat.

"Yeah, yeah," Jem said, waving his hand like my talk was boring him, "that's what *she* says anyway." He stood and began clapping in a thunderous manner as Buffalo Bill charged by on his horse, followed by ten Indians in full feathered **headdresses.**

For three whole hours, we watched in awe as the Wild West scenes unfolded before our eyes. We witnessed one drama after another come to life, all so real I barely remembered to speak or even breathe. Hardly a word passed between us all the way through to the last moments of the final grand spectacle. That was the defeat of General Custer at Little Bighorn. As it ended, I let loose a sigh of complete satisfaction. What a show I'd seen!

The other reason I'd barely spoken was that I was still stewing over everything Jem had said about Annie. It just made me angry how dumb a brother he could be sometimes, and that anger got my tongue, for sure.

As we worked our way out of the arena with the rest of the crowd, I couldn't keep silent any longer though. Looking up, I saw that mighty new **contraption** that was causing so much excited talk at the fair. It stood just a short ways off in the amusement area called the Midway Plaisance. A giant wheel looming into the heavens.

The Ferris wheel was invented by George W. Ferris, a bridge builder from Pittsburgh, Pennsylvania.

"Look, Jem, the Ferris wheel! Can we ride it?"

"That thing would scare the dickens out of you, Tay," he laughed.

"Would not!" I kicked a stone and scowled, trying to keep up with his long-legged steps.

At the Columbian Exposition, each Ferris wheel ride cost 50 cents. By the end of the fair, the ride had brought in $726,805.50.

"And anyway, I got some business in Bill Cody's camp."

"What business?" I asked suspiciously.

We'd been heading back that way as we talked, toward the show's encampment. That was the area where all the Wild West performers stayed in between the afternoon show and the evening show. Sure I wanted to see what it was like for myself. But I couldn't imagine my brother having an appointment there or any such thing. No matter how many strings he could pull to get his way, I sorely doubted that meeting up with Colonel Cody was something Jem had managed to arrange.

With a few confident words to the right people though, he had us passing into the campground, no problem. The next minute we were part of the **bustling** activity behind the scenes. It was a spectacle there, too, with nearly as many fascinating sights to see as the real show. I saw a group of folks seated on barrels, playing banjos and harmonicas. Men brushing down horses and repairing wagons. Indians playing cards with men dressed as bandits. Three beautiful brown-skinned girls in fancy clothing passed by on horseback, laughing happily. Someone led a buffalo across our path on a **tether.**

"Jem!" I exclaimed, truly excited to be in the midst of it all. "This is great! Where are we going?"

The Ferris wheel was huge!

One reason Buffalo Bill got his nickname was for killing buffalo. But by using a number of them in his show, he actually helped keep the buffalo from dying out.

All kinds of people visited Chicago that summer and enjoyed the Columbian Exposition.

Jem had been walking quickly in front of me, moving like he knew exactly where he had to get to. Hearing me, he turned abruptly and stopped. There was a slightly surprised look on his face, as if he'd forgotten I was with him.

"Oh yeah," he said then. "The Tag-Along. What am I going to do with the Tag-Along?" He scratched his head. His lips gathered together into a tight little knot of annoyance. It was clear he was trying to figure out where to park me while he took care of his business.

That's when it hit me bad. His face, looking so bothered at having me there, that stone around his neck, just did it. Like a wave of seasickness, something bad came

One of the Wild West Show performers

Annie Oakley relaxing after a show

rising up into my whole body. I could feel it gagging my throat, like I might throw up. I could feel a burning behind my eyes, like stupid tears might be trying to get out.

I didn't move for what seemed a long, long moment, and neither did Jem. We just stood there looking at each other. Then I turned and ran.

I ran fast. I didn't know where I was going, but I ran like my feet didn't dare touch the ground. I ran through crowds of people, zigzagged between covered wagons and fancy **stagecoaches.** I ran past a long table where dozens of surprised-looking folks were dishing up food. I ran so fast that the wind in my eyes kept any stray tears from escaping. I ran until I could no longer hear

Jem shouting out my name. Until I had lost the sound of his pounding footsteps behind me. Until I hadn't another breath left to breathe. Then I collapsed.

I didn't faint, but I was so weak and my **limbs** so rubbery that I just clean dropped to the ground on my knees. A few sound-less tears streaked my dusty face, and the heat of the summer afternoon trickled down my back. I wiped my nose with the back of my hand and looked around. I was behind a large tent, but still some folks were passing by. I got up quickly, before any of them could offer to help me or ask me what was wrong.

In the tree shade at the backside of the tent, I noticed an old leather trunk. I moved that way and sat down there to rest a while, hoping I could figure out what to do. I'd really done it to myself, I thought. Now I didn't have a single clue how to find Jem again. But who wanted to find him anyhow? No doubt he'd chased me for a good ten seconds and then been happy to be rid of his burden. Right now, in fact, he was probably signing on with the Wild West Show, with not even a care about what was to become of me.

Not that I'd ever mentioned it to him, but Jem wasn't the only one who wanted to get that Wild West job. Maybe I couldn't shoot like Annie Oakley, but I could ride. I could ride good and hard and fast. I'd prac-ticed many hours before we'd had to leave Aspen. I could even keep perfect balance while standing on the saddle of a galloping horse. Just as good as any of those girls I'd seen earlier in the show, too, so why couldn't I be one of them?

I dusted off my skirt and buttoned up an undone button on one of my leggings. Then I closed my eyes, praying for a sign of what to do next. I couldn't tell how much time had passed like that when someone spoke to me. Her voice was cheery and soft, like a sweet melody.

"Why, hello there," the voice said. "Are you all right?" I opened my eyes.

The sun was lowering in the sky behind her, so I could only see the outline of her form at first. All the details of her face or other features were thrown into shade. But the sun's golden rays shone all around her, bathing her in a **halo** of light. *An angel!* I thought. *An angel come to save me!*

Then she stepped closer and as she did, the shade lifted from her face and I saw her clearly. I knew then that an angel had indeed come to save me. Her name was Annie Oakley.

Oakley was nicknamed "Little Sure Shot" by Sitting Bull, a famous Native American chief who considered her his adopted daughter.

"Oh, Miss Oakley!" I said, straightening up. "I'm so sorry! I don't mean to be bothering anyone. Especially you."

She laughed gently. "No bother at all," she said, with a fair twinkle in her eye. "Have you got a name?"

"Taylor Virginia Blackwell, ma'am."

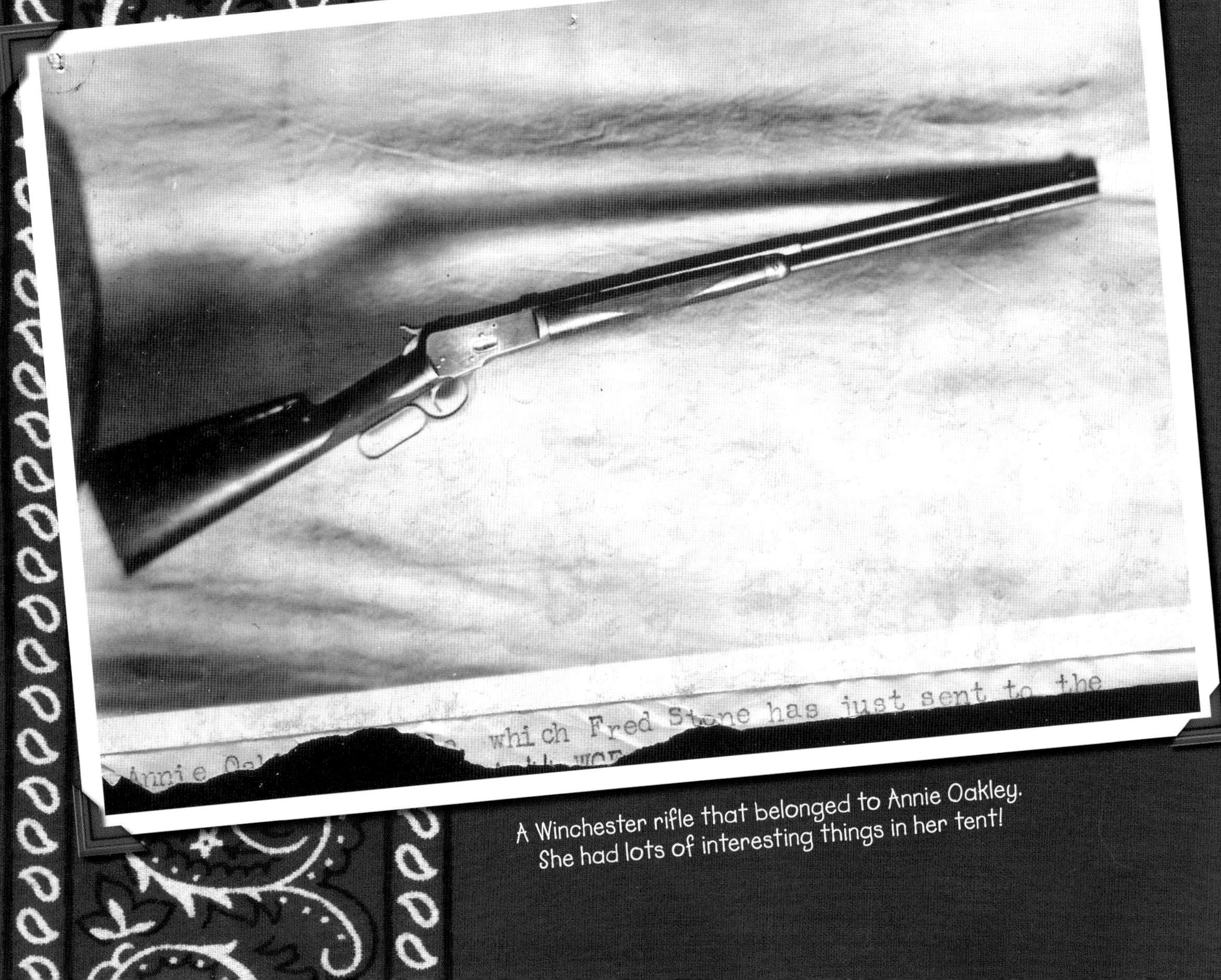


A Winchester rifle that belonged to Annie Oakley.
She had lots of interesting things in her tent!

"Taylor," Annie repeated. "I reckon that's an excellent name for a girl."

"Thank you, ma'am," I replied. "Most people think it's only for boys, but it was my mama's last name before she married my daddy and I'm happy to have it."

"And well you should be. There are plenty enough things in this world that—with no good reason—belong only to boys. But neither names nor good **marksmanship** have to be one of them, right?"

I nodded, relieved to find her as friendly as I'd heard she was.

"Now, why don't you come around to my tent and have something nice and cool to drink with me?" Annie invited.

Annie Oakley met her husband at a shooting competition. He lost to her.

Speechless, I could only nod. She led me around the corner and I found I'd been sitting behind her very own tent. The next moment I was seated in a rocking chair inside the most wonderful place in the world, an ice-cold lemonade in hand. Annie explained to me that she and her husband, Frank Butler, stayed in a nice hotel nearby, but during the day she had her tent for resting and writing and entertaining visitors.

After the bustle and humid heat outside, coming into Annie's tent was like entering a museum. There was a cool hush to the air and several vases of flowers gave off the sweet scent of a garden. Beneath my feet, the ground was covered in a soft, floral-patterned carpet. Photographs and paintings of every sort hung from the tent's canvas walls, and in one corner I spied a number of fancy, gleaming rifles lined up one after another. But the best feature of all was Annie's collection of sharp-shooting medals that she'd won all over the world. Some of them she wore pinned to the **bodice** of her dress, but she showed me many, many more, describing where and how she had won her most favorite ones.

Finally, Annie said, "Enough of all that. What about you, Miss Taylor?"

What about *me*? I regretted that the conversation had turned to me and my sorry situation. I started slowly, but with a little coaxing, Annie soon had the whole story flying

The snow in Colorado could be pretty, but our last winter there was a terrible one.

from my lips. I began by telling her about the terrible never-ending snows the winter before in Colorado, which she had heard news of. Then I went on to describe the disaster that had taken our parents, and soon my entire tale of woe was tumbling out. It flowed with all the force of a stream that had been dammed and ready to burst for way too long.

Finally I had drained it all. I finished with what had just happened earlier. I described how I had run from Jem, hoping in that moment never to see him again.

"He's going to get a job with Colonel Cody and just leave me to my own fate!" I cried at last.

"Hmmph!" Annie said. "We'll just see about that. How would you like to be a cowgirl here in the show yourself, Taylor? You could get your schooling on the road, like the other young'uns. I'm sure the Colonel would have you, if you tried out well."

Though earlier I had been so sure of myself, the moment Annie actually suggested the possibility, I shrank.

"Oh, I couldn't possibly!" I said. "I'm not that good. And anyway, Jem would just laugh at me if I even tried!"

Annie leaned forward with the kindest look I'd ever seen since I last laid eyes on my ma.

"You listen here," she said. "A girl can do anything in the world she sets her mind to. Don't pay a moment's notice to any fool boy who's going to try to keep you down!"

Horses and other animals played a big part in the Wild West Show.

She sat back and sipped her lemonade. It was clear why all who met her found her so strong and sure, and yet so ladylike and charming at the same time.

"I wouldn't have a single medal today if I hadn't had a mind of my own to go after it," Annie went on. "That's to say, can you imagine how far I'd have gotten if I had listened to every man who ever said I couldn't do this or that? Or to all those who tried to make me feel it wasn't right for a woman to do a 'man's business'?"

"Not far, I guess," I admitted.

"Not far at all. Only one reason I've succeeded so well as a markswoman. It's because I heartily believed I could do it. Kept my confidence up and my doubts as far off my back as I could."

In his show, Buffalo Bill used men and women, girls and boys, from a variety of backgrounds. For his time, he was very open-minded and accepting of all sorts of people.

"Yes," I said, "but you have a talent. It comes second nature to you."

"We've all got talent, Taylor. If you really want to be an ace rider in the show, well then, you put your whole mind to it and see if you don't just succeed."

"Do you really think I could?" Annie's calm, firm assurances were like a strengthening **tonic** to my heart and mind.

"Of course you can! It may take a few missed shots before you hit the **bull's-eye,** so to speak. But it can surely be done. The key is, don't you let anybody—no boy especially—plant a single thought of failure in your head."

I nodded, just barely beginning to accept the possibility that I might be able to earn success in something special myself.

"Now, we should probably go about trying to find that brother of yours, don't you think?" Annie said then.

Before I could answer, the sound of boot steps and clinking spurs came to my ears. The next moment all six feet, two inches of Buffalo Bill Cody stood in the doorway of Annie's tent. Jem was standing just behind him. I shot to my feet, barely believing it.

Annie Oakley was in a train wreck in 1901 and never fully recovered. She left Buffalo Bill's Wild West Show the following year.

A portrait of Annie Oakley

Buffalo Bill Cody was friends with Theodore Roosevelt, leader of the Rough Riders during the Spanish-American War and later president of the United States.

Buffalo Bill came looking for me and found me in Annie's tent.

"Missie!" Colonel Cody boomed, looking in at Annie. "We've got a lost orphan wandering somewhere around these parts. Will you help me gather the troops to find her? This here's her brother." He jabbed a thumb back Jem's way.

"Jem!" I exclaimed.

"Tay?!" came Jem's surprised reply. He stepped forward into the doorway of the tent and saw me standing beside Annie's chair. There was a moment of hesitation, and then he rushed in. Jem grabbed me and hugged me tight, like I was something more dear and precious to him than I'd ever believed possible. And in my ear, the words of his apologies sounded real and heartfelt to the core. Just hearing those words from my brother made everything seem suddenly right and the world once again safe.

"You see, Colonel," Annie said, getting up from her chair and gracing Buffalo Bill with a calm, sweet smile. "I've already done the job."

"As usual," Buffalo Bill said, with a wide grin.

I rode in Buffalo Bill's Wild West Show at the World's Fair all that summer of '93 and all the way through October 31, the day the fair closed. And then some after that, too, in other parts of the world. Every time I got up in that saddle before the crowd, I could hear Annie's wise words in my head.

"Fire away before you have time to doubt the certainty of success," she'd told me, and I knew that didn't apply just to shooting. It applied to any little thing I might want to do in life. More than anything else, Annie had taught me that success came by not letting the doubts get in.

Author Mark Twain encouraged Buffalo Bill to take his show to Europe in 1887, so Europeans could see something "truly American."

Jem finally got a job in the show too, of course. But he'd gone through a few things with Colonel Cody before that job was for sure. For instance, he got **railed** upon when he suggested that a man should get more pay than a woman, even if she was doing the same exact job he was. Buffalo Bill was having none of that, oh no. Like Annie—and me, too—he believed in equal pay for men and women both. He was **righteously** annoyed at what he considered my brother's ignorant viewpoint on that matter. Which turned Jem around some, to be sure.

They got into it over a woman's right to vote in national elections, too. Buffalo Bill said it was just a matter of time until that happened, but Jem said it was the dumbest thing he'd ever heard. He didn't believe in it at all, until Colonel Cody took the opportunity to wise him up good. All in all, it was a while before Jem smartened up about such things. But under the influence of Bill Cody, his number-one hero, he finally did.

Women finally obtained the right to vote in 1920, the year the Nineteenth Amendment went into effect.

At one of our last performances in Chicago, I persuaded Bill to set up a new race for the cowgirls to try. It took some doing, but he finally agreed. Seven of us came in together, me in the lead on a mighty black stallion, all dressed in white. After we circled the arena doing our most daring tricks, a band of seven cowboys charged in to join us. We raced them, one end of the arena to the other, all the folks watching us screaming like crazy.

Jem was in that race. I beat him, too. With the wind whipping through my hair, my horse on the fly, I turned and looked back. He was riding hard trying to catch up.

A joyous rush exploded inside my heart. All around us the sound of the crowd was added thunder to the beat of horse hooves.

"Come on, Jem!" I shouted back at him, laughing. "You better move it! *You Tag-Along!*"

He was some yards behind, but I heard it clearly when he laughed, too. It was a genuinely happy sound, not his mean laugh from the old days. Hearing his laughter now gladdened my heart. We'd come a long way from Aspen, to be sure. And as it turned out, I had a brother who wasn't half bad after all.

For a Tag-Along, that is.

A poster for the fair. My whole life changed the day I visited the Columbian Exposition and saw the Wild West Show.

You could tell that Buffalo Bill's performers were having fun.

# THE HISTORY OF ANNIE OAKLEY AND BUFFALO BILL'S WILD WEST SHOW

In the spring of 1893, twelve-year-old Taylor Blackwell and her brother Jeremiah attended Buffalo Bill Cody's Wild West Show in Chicago, Illinois. The traveling show, which toured the United States and parts of Europe, was a popular attraction at the Columbian Exposition. It ran from May 1st to October 31st.

The show grounds, located near the train tracks on the west side of the fair grounds, included indoor and outdoor arenas, campgrounds with an authentic Indian village, a frontier cabin, circus tents, and stables for more than 400 horses, bison, and elk.

Elaborate productions showcased the talents and experiences of Buffalo Bill Cody and friends. A bison hunt, train robbery, stagecoach hold-up, and reenactment of the battle at the Little Bighorn resembled scenes from Cody's own life on the frontier. The cast, which included hundreds of people, highlighted the skills of Native Americans and brought together some of the finest sharpshooters and horsemen from the United States, England, France, Germany, Russia, Mexico, and South America.

Phoebe Ann Mosey (or Moses), whose stage name was Annie Oakley, was a featured sharpshooter in the show. Especially popular with women, Ms. Mosey dazzled audiences with her ability to shoot a dime out of a person's hand or a cigarette out of a person's mouth. Ms. Mosey joined the show in 1884 and remained with the cast until she was injured in a train accident in 1901.

William Frederick Cody and friends formed "Buffalo Bill's Wild West" show in 1883 and advertised it as "a living picture of life on the frontier." The show, however, provided an unrealistic view of the West. Actually, by 1883 the bison was nearly extinct, most Native American tribes had been defeated in battle and confined to reservations, and Mexicans had been driven out of the southwestern United States. The show continued to provide an exaggerated picture of frontier life, even after it was sold in 1913. Remarkably, the Wild West Show was the most successful traveling entertainment of the late 1800s.

## GLOSSARY

**annoyance** something that makes a person feel angry or impatient

**archangels** members of the highest order of angels

**arena** a large area used for sports and entertainment

**avalanches** large masses of snow and ice that suddenly move down a mountain

**boardinghouse** a home where rooms are rented and meals provided

**bodice** the upper part of a woman's dress

**buckskin** a strong, soft material made from the skin of a deer or sheep

**bull's-eye** the center of a target

**bustling** filled with people rushing around and being busy

**congress** the meeting or coming together of a group; the term is also used to refer to the legislative branch of government

**contraption** a strange or odd device or machine

**drawled** spoke in a slow manner

**exhibits** displays that are shown to the public

## TIMELINE

**1846** William Frederick Cody, later known as Buffalo Bill, is born on February 26 in Scott County, Iowa.

**1860** The Pony Express begins service and operates a mail route between Missouri and California; Annie Oakley is born on August 13 in Darke County, Ohio.

**1861–1865** The Civil War rages as a result of the debate over slavery.

**1871** The Great Chicago Fire destroys much of the city.

**1876** George Custer is defeated at the Battle of the Little Bighorn, later known as Custer's Last Stand.

**1883** Buffalo Bill Cody organizes Buffalo Bill's Wild West Show.

**halo** a ring of light around something or someone

**headdresses** decorative coverings for the head

**herd** a large group of animals

**hurrah** excitement and fanfare

**limbs** parts of the body used in moving and grasping, such as arms and legs

**marksmanship** the sport of shooting at a mark or target with precision

**markswoman** a woman who is expert at shooting a gun

**railed** scolded excitedly

**righteously** in a just manner, with good reason

**sabers** large swords with curved blades

**stagecoaches** carriages pulled by horses and used to transport people over long distances

**suffocating** causing someone to have difficulty breathing

**tether** a rope or chain used to tie an animal

**tonic** something, like a medicine, that helps a person feel stronger or refreshed

**1892–1893** Residents of Aspen, Colorado, experience a difficult winter filled with often fatal snowstorms.

**1893** The Columbian Exposition takes place in Chicago.

**1902** Annie Oakley leaves the Wild West Show, a year after being injured in a train accident.

**1917** Buffalo Bill Cody dies on January 10 in Denver, Colorado.

**1920** The Nineteenth Amendment, which granted women the right to vote, is finally approved.

**1926** Annie Oakley dies on November 3 in Greenville, Ohio.

ACTIVITIES

## Continuing the Story

*(Writing Creatively)*

Continue Tay's story. Elaborate on an event from her scrapbook or add your own entries to the beginning or end of her journal. You might write about her experiences as a young female performer in the Wild West Show and her relationship with Annie Oakley. Or you can write your own short story of historical fiction about the Wild West Show, basing it on a set of cast members that you create to tour with the Show.

## Celebrating Your Heritage

*(Discovering Family History)*

Research your own family history. Find out if you had any relatives attending the 1893 Columbian Exposition. Were they living in Chicago, Illinois, at the time or visiting from out of town? Were your relatives involved directly or indirectly with the Wild West Show or the Columbian Exposition as cast members, stagehands, or laborers? Ask family members to write down what they know about the people and events of this time period. Make copies of old photographs or drawings of keepsakes that you collect from this era.

## Documenting History

*(Exploring Community History)*

Explore your community's involvement in Buffalo Bill Cody's Wild West Show and the Columbian Exposition of 1893. Visit your library, a historical society, a museum, or related Web sites for links to important people and events. What did newspapers report at the time? When, where, why, and how did your community respond? Who was involved? What was the result?

## Preserving Memories

*(Crafting)*

Make a scrapbook about family life in Chicago during the 1890s, or the family life of cast members participating in the Wild West Show. Fill the pages with special events, family stories, interviews with relatives, letters, and drawings of family treasures. Include copies of newspaper clippings, photos, posters, postcards, and historical records. Decorate the pages and cover with family heirlooms, train schedules, souvenir tickets, booklets, and posters from the Wild West Show.

# TO FIND OUT MORE

## At the Library

Green, Carl R. *Buffalo Bill Cody: Showman of the Wild West.* Berkeley Heights, N.J.: Enslow, 1996.

Kimmel, Elizabeth Cody. *One Sky above Us.* New York: HarperCollins, 2002.

Shields, Charles J. *Annie Oakley.* Broomall, Pa.: Chelsea House, 2001.

## On the Internet

**The Annie Oakley Foundation**
*http://www.ormiston.com/annieoakley*
To learn more about Annie Oakley's life

**The Cast of the Wild West Show**
*http://xroads.virginia.edu/~HYPER/HNS/BuffaloBill/billcast.html*
To learn about the kinds of people who took part in the performances

**National Cowboy and Western Heritage Museum**
*http://www.cowboyhalloffame.org*
For a virtual tour of the museum

**New Perspectives on the West: William F. Cody**
*http://www.pbs.org/weta/thewest/people/a_c/cody.htm*
For a biography of Buffalo Bill

# Places to Visit

**Buffalo Bill's Grave and Museum**
987-1/2 Lookout Mountain Road
Golden, CO 80401
303/526-0747
*To learn more about Buffalo Bill's life through artifacts from his life*

**Buffalo Bill Historical Center**
720 Sheridan Avenue
Cody, WY 82414
307/587-4771
*To visit the Buffalo Bill museum and other museums in the historical center*

**Garst Museum**
205 North Broadway
Greenville, OH 45331
937/548-5250
*To see the largest collection of Annie Oakley artifacts*

**National Women's Hall of Fame**
76 Fall Street
Seneca falls, NY 13148
315/568-8060
*To learn more about Annie Oakley and other brave and famous women*

## ABOUT THE AUTHOR

Pamela Dell has been making her living as a writer for about fifteen years. Though she has published both fiction and nonfiction for adults, in the last decade she has written mostly for kids. Her nonfiction work includes biographies, science, history, and nature topics. She has also published contemporary and historical fiction, as well as award-winning interactive multimedia. The twelve books in the Scrapbooks of America series have been some of her favorite writing projects.